F
HUR

Hurwitz, Johanna

Class clown

$10.25

F
HUR

Hurwitz, Johanna
Class clown

DATE DUE	BORROWER'S NAME	ROOM NUMBER
5-10	Jennifer Malmg	4-12
1-18	Nicky	
9-7	Stephanie	5-H